We Can Do It!

We Can Do It!

Dawn McCuin

gatekeeper press™
Columbus, OH

We Can Do It!
Published by Gatekeeper Press
2167 Stringtown Rd, Suite 109
Columbus, OH 43123-2989
www.GatekeeperPress.com

Library of Congress Control Number: 2021938471

ISBN (hardcover): 9781662913204

ISBN (paperback): 9781662913211

eISBN: 9781662913228

To my beautiful girls, you inspire me everyday. I hope that I inspire you!

Love, Mommy

"Raven, what are you doing up so early?" Mama asked as she walked into the kitchen. "You should be getting ready for school, baby."

"Yeah, I know, Mama," Raven replied, "but I've been working on a new project."

"What is it?" Mama asked.

"A volcano!" Raven announced. "When it erupts, candy will spew out instead of lava!"

Mama smiled as Raven continued to explain.

"The fifth-grade science fair is coming up soon. Last year I got third place. This year, I know I can do better."

"You're always up to something," Mama said, a grin spreading across her kind face. "I'm sure your volcano is going to be great. But you really need to get ready for school, okay, baby?"

Raven nodded as her mother turned to leave.

KABOOM!

The volcano erupted with a loud pop. It spewed colorful wet goo across the kitchen floor.

"Oh *nooooo*," Raven grunted. "I definitely added too much water. It's supposed to be mostly candy that comes out when the volcano erupts."

The gooey mess was all over the floor, but the table was clean.

Raven smiled. "It's so close to being perfect."

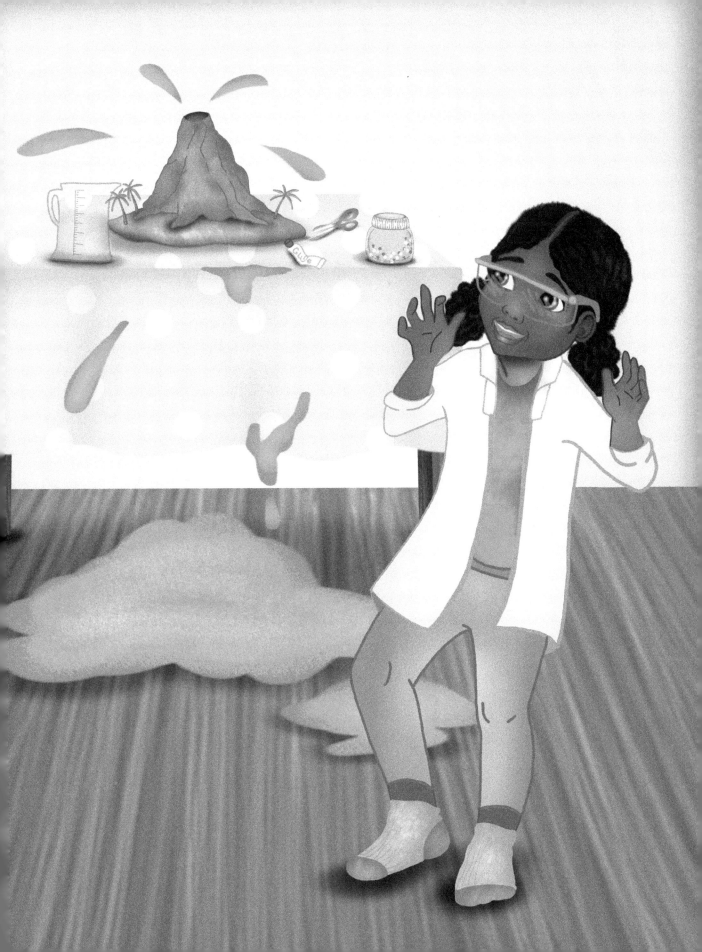

She turned at the sound of a familiar voice. Russell, her brother, was standing in the doorway, laughing and pointing.

"Girls can't invent stuff," he chuckled. "I still remember that thing you made last year. The hat that kept blinking on and off, right?"

"Yeah, I guess," Raven answered.

"Oh, and who could forget the personal vending machine the year before that?" he added. "When it exploded, the mess got all over the principal! This time, it's all over our kitchen floor."

Raven sighed. Her brother's memory was on the mark. But she wasn't about to take his teasing quietly.

"Oh, kind of like how red marks were all over your pre-algebra test last week? Seventh grade is eating you alive," Raven quickly responded with a smirk.

"Yeah, whatever, we'll see how you do once you're out of elementary school," Russell said as he rolled his eyes.

He grabbed some paper towels off the counter and handed them to his sister.

"I can dream," Raven declared. "Maybe one day I'll build a time machine."

"Really, Raven?" her brother snickered. "You?"

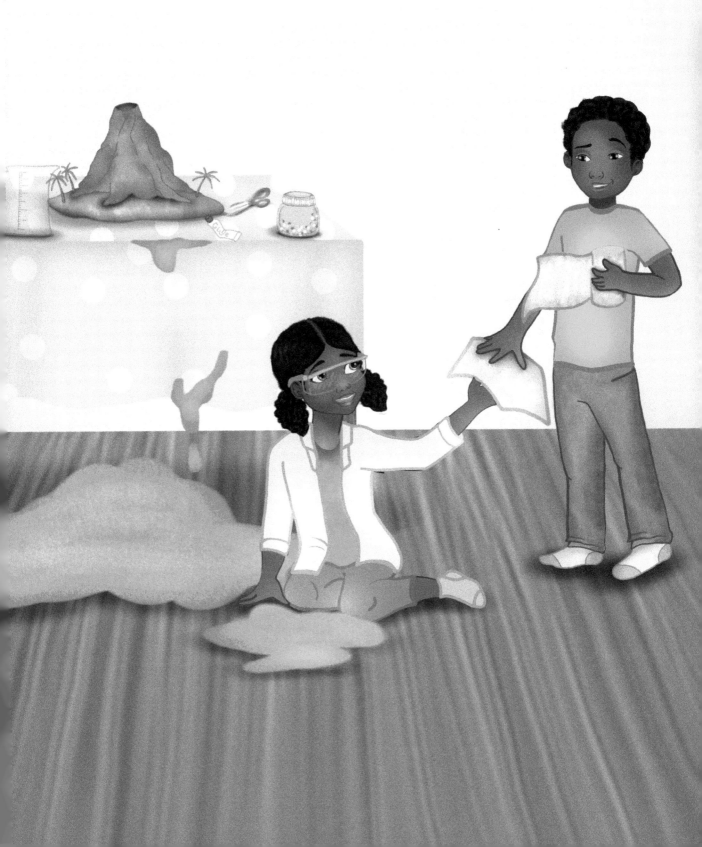

"Yes, ME!" Raven exclaimed, as she used a towel to wipe the messy floor. "I might invent a remote control that makes tasty treats. I could figure out how to make flying cars. Or maybe I'll build robots that do unimaginable things!"

Russell crossed his arms. "Yeah, sure. But like I said before, girls can't invent stuff."

Raven frowned at her brother's words.

"Have you ever heard of Madam C. J. Walker?" she asked as she looked up at him. "She was the daughter of slaves and lost her parents when she was a kid. She made products that could help Black women grow healthy hair. They worked well. She opened a beauty school and a factory, and she became one of the first Black female self-made millionaires in America," Raven explained.

"Good for her, I guess," said Russell with a shrug, "but only girls care about hair. Who else you got?"

Raven took a moment to think. "Oh! There was Maria Van Brittan Brown. She was a nurse."

"I thought we were talking about inventing stuff?" Russell said, tilting his head and looking a bit puzzled.

"I'll get to that!" Raven snapped. "You see, Maria and her husband lived in a rough neighborhood. They both worked a lot and at different times of the day. Maria was often home late without him. Crime was bad and the local cops weren't all that great."

"That sounds awful," Russell almost whispered. "What did she do?"

"She found a way to watch people walking by her apartment and look out for unexpected visitors. That idea became . . ." Raven's voice trailed off as she pointed to a spot on the wall near the door to their backyard.

Russell's eyes widened with surprise as his sister announced, ". . . the home alarm security system! Yes, a Black woman invented the home alarm system during a time when many African Americans were fighting for basic civil rights."

"Okay," Russell said, nodding his head, "so that's *two girls* who made things. Congratulations." He snickered as he turned to leave the kitchen.

"Hold on! Make that three," Raven said as she followed her brother. "Alice H. Parker invented the first thermostat."

"What?"

Raven pulled him to a window in the living room. She pointed to the thermostat mounted on the wall.

"Why did she do it?" Russell asked.

Raven began slowly. "Well, chopping wood took a lot of time and energy. And fireplaces weren't always the safest."

"I see," Russell said. "So, her invention made heating a house more convenient?"

"And efficient! You got it," said Raven. "Alice H. Parker managed to file a patent as a woman during a time when women were fighting for the right to vote and many African Americans were facing obstacles like segregation. Blacks and Whites went to separate schools. They actually had to drink from separate water fountains. In many places, they could not even live in the same neighborhoods. Alice Parker's invention wasn't just efficient, it was revolutionary!" said Raven.

Russell glanced up at the clock.

"Whoa, segregation sounds horrible! Raven, you've been talking my ear off. I need to iron my shirt before we go to school," Russell said as he hurried across the living room.

"Guess what? I'm going to keep on talking."

Russell set up the ironing board. Raven grabbed the iron for her brother. She plugged it in and set it down on the board.

"Sarah Boone invented the ironing board. However, her life began as a slave in the 1800s," Raven continued. "At that time, many African Americans were considered property. They were forced to work doing whatever their masters wanted. They often lived in horrible conditions," she explained.

"Luckily, Sarah obtained her freedom through marriage and she became an inventor. We should all be grateful," Raven said. "People used to use a wooden plank. Ironing across it was difficult."

Fig.1

"*Hmm*," hummed Russell as he slid the iron across his shirt. "She made this job easier, huh?"

"Much easier," Raven laughed. "You can thank her for making sure you don't look like a hot mess every day!"

Russell sighed. His sister was right about that.

He flipped his shirt to iron the other side.

"Can you think of any more inventors?" Russell asked. "I'm listening."

Raven looked across the room at the sofa, a big smile spreading across her face.

"Sarah Goode. She was also born into slavery. She got her freedom after the Civil War," Raven explained. "Sarah made furniture for people who lived in small spaces. She invented a bed that could also fold into a desk. She was one of the first African American women to receive a patent in the United States. A patent gives an inventor the right to stop other people from making or using their invention without permission," she added.

"Hey, I could use something like that," Russell chuckled.

Satisfied with his freshly ironed shirt, he glanced at the clock one last time.

"Raven, can I look at your volcano before we go to school?" he asked with a kind smile. "Maybe I can help in some way."

"Really?" Raven replied, her face lighting up.

"Yeah, sure," Russell said. "You've convinced me."

"Convinced you of what?"

"That girls really can invent anything they put their minds to," he said, lightly resting his hand on his sister's shoulder.

Then Russell's voice got serious.

"Raven, you're going to absolutely blow the judges away this year," he said. "All those women you told me about did amazing things. I know that you'll do something just as amazing, or better!"

Resources to Learn More

Books

1. Rebel Girls. *Madam C.J. Walker Builds a Business (A Good Night Stories for Rebel Girls Chapter Book)*. Rebel Girls, 2019.

2. Bundles, A'Lelia. *All About Madam C.J. Walker*. Blue River Press,. 2020.

3. Loh-Hagan, Virginia. *Marie Van Brittan Brown and Home Security*. Cherry Lake Publishing, 2018.

4. Loh-Hagan, Virginia. *Alice H. Parker and the Furnace*. Cherry Lake Publishing, 2018.

5. Kirkfield, Vivian. *Sweet Dreams, Sarah: From Slavery to Inventor*. Creston Books, 2019.

Websites

1. NAACP.org
2. Biography.com
3. Brittanica.com
4. Encyclopedia.com

CPSIA information can be obtained
at www.ICGtesting.com
Printed in the USA
LVHW070339150122
708631LV00002B/8

9 781662 913204